4/14

EssexWorks.

fe

D0625968

561962

2 3 OCT 2014

For Charley, Dan and Annie

JANETTA OTTER-BARRY BOOKS

Text and illustrations copyright © Kathy Henderson 2013
The right of Kathy Henderson to be identified as the author and illustrator
of this work has been asserted by her in accordance with the Copyright,
Designs and Patents Act, 1988 (United Kingdom).

First published in Great Britain in 2013 by
Frances Lincoln Children's Books,
74-77 White Lion Street, London N1 9PF
www.franceslincoln.com

A catalogue record for this book is available from the British Library.

ISBN 978-1-84780-365-8

Set in Sabon

Printed and bound by CPI Group
(UK) Ltd, Croydon, CR0 4YY

3 5 7 9 8 6 4 2

THE DRAGON
WITH A
BIG NOSE

Poems and drawings by
Kathy Henderson

F
FRANCES LINCOLN
CHILDREN'S BOOKS

Contents

Today I read a bus stop

Today I read a bus stop
and then I read a van,
a poster and three carrier bags,
some shop signs and a man
who had a crazy T-shirt on.

I'd already read the cereal box,
a mug, and the jam label
and the headlines of the paper
that was lying on the table.

I read some writing in the sky,
I even read the road,

a tree, a sign stuck in the grass,
some number plates that whistled past,

a bag of crisps, a birthday card,
(it had my name on it so that was easy).

amazing

I was reading a text message
when I should have read the door
so then I pushed instead of pulled
and dropped my mobile on the floor.

Then I started on this poem
and went out for another look

because

reading is amazing
and all the world's a book.

This is the city

This is the city:
buildings, buses, trains and cars
concrete, metal, bricks and glass
houses, lights and cinemas
shops and offices and bars
this is where the people are.
This is the city.

Out in the city

Out in the city what can you see?

A mother with a baby much smaller than me
    riding on her back
    in a big striped sash
and a boy talking a language I don't understand.

There's a man with a fiddle and magic hands
playing tunes that make my feet get up and dance

and another with his hair in a cockatoo's crest
and rings in his nose and his ear and his lip

and a woman covered from head to toe
just her eyes looking out through a cloth window

and right in the middle of all those streets
I saw a girl who was walking a sheep.

Home again and shut the door.
Tomorrow we'll go out and see some more.

Where we grow up

Where we grow up
the cats grow faster
the holes in the road
and the cracks in the plaster
and all around the traffic sings.

Somewhere
the people must be sleeping on new beds
because here are all their old ones dumped
in the alleys and the yards,
leaking mattresses and rusty springs.

Listen.
Go out of the back door
into the night
and beyond the yowling
of the cruising cats
you will hear
    near
    behind walls
lots of other people

breathing.

Walking down the pavement

Walking down the pavement
watch where you tread
if you step on a drain lid
you might bump your head.

Walking down the pavement
splashing in the rain
if you step on a kerb stone
you'll go down the drain.

Kerb stones

Marking time,
holding the line
down every street
in this town

there are
kerb stones
hard stones
out of the ground stones
cut into slabs
the corner keepers.

They are the edge.
They divide
the people from the cars
our place from their place
and this street from centuries of still rock.

They guard the gutters
They are
      crash barriers
      wheel bashers
      rubbish catchers
      riverbanks on rainy days
      fences lying down

and we tread them underfoot.

The dragon with a big nose

The dragon with a big nose
and twelve toes
on each foot,
eats flies
and mince pies

and sometimes,
when he's very bad,
whole towns
upside down,

streets and houses,
shops and churches,
schools and factories,
undergrounds,

swallows them all
quite whole
and spits out the glass
   fast
      treading very carefully
      somewhere else
      going away.

No one's ever seen him coming.
They can't see him leave.
No one's ever seen him anyway

     . . . except me.

The gutter creature

The
gutter creature
rustles litter,
chews up paper bags
      and old packets of crisps.

When you think you're alone
     or you start to dream
          along the road
     it kicks
     tin cans
up against the kerb stones

and starts to chase
with the wind in its wings,
     flapping,
crumpled newspaper ghost.

Cats stalk it
dogs scuffle it
but
one look and it's gone,
slithered in strips
through the bars of a drain
chuckling in the rain.

Milkman

Early morning
the first hum
is the milkman's float
on its battery run
chattering the bottles
down our street
while we're still asleep.

Dustcart dragon

Dustmen's wagon
raging rusty belly
comes to gorge outside the window
in the early morning.
It whines,
it roars and crunches,
gnashes
trash and rubbish
with rows and rows of steel teeth
in its iron jaws,
smoke pouring.

Behind closed doors
we
block our ears,
put pillows over our heads,
hold our noses,
turn over in bed
and hide.

Leaving the men with the leather shoulders
to feed the monster with our leftovers,
dustcart dragon.

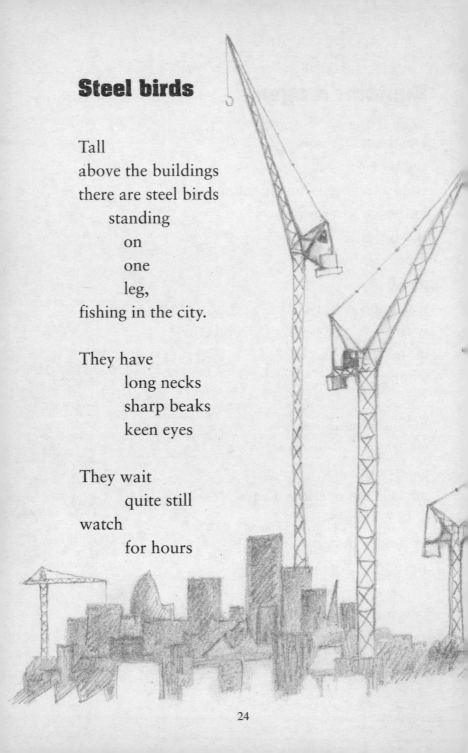

Steel birds

Tall
above the buildings
there are steel birds
   standing
      on
      one
       leg,
fishing in the city.

They have
     long necks
     sharp beaks
     keen eyes

They wait
     quite still
watch
     for hours

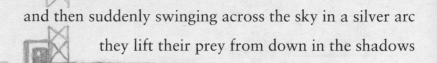

and then suddenly swinging across the sky in a silver arc

they lift their prey from down in the shadows

concrete beams
iron girders
heaps of bricks
half roofs
machines

And
having raised them carefully up
and gulped them down
they
go
back
to
stand
-ing
watch
-ing
on
the skyline.

Street light

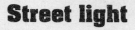

On the pavement
in front of our house
stands a one-legged watchman
tall
still
biding its time.

All day long
people lean on it
dogs sniff at it
small bikes crash into it
and litter gathers round it
in the roadside wind.

Doing nothing
in the way
it's a dull
grey
pole
biding its time

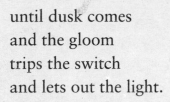

until dusk comes
and the gloom
trips the switch
and lets out the light.

Outside my window then
the swan-necked silver street light
shines through the night.

A house is

A house is like a skin
for keeping people in
and the weather out ...
just about.

When it rains

When it rains
they put their heads down
        and walk faster
but I
want to stand still,
   look up
and see the drops
   falling.

When it rains
they say
'Put your hood up.'
'Keep under here.'
and
'Don't get your feet wet.'

but I
want to walk
  in the puddles,
feel my feet squelching
  in my shoes
and hear the gutter water
wash a tide of rubbish
  down the hill.

When it rains
they say
'Hurry up.
We're going home.'
and
'Do hurry up!'

but I
want to stop
and watch the windscreen wipers
  setting up a dance
and forests of umbrellas
  springing up
and buses throwing fountains
  at our legs.

Then they say
'Come in.'
and
'Wipe your feet.'
and louder
'Shut the door!'
but I
want to stay
   outside
and feel the rain fall,
let my hair
turn into rats-tails round my ears
and smell the bushes
   drinking up the wet.

Summer is coming

Summer is coming
the rain is teeming wet
you'll have to put your brolly up
if you're going out.

If you haven't got a brolly, a raincoat will do
If you haven't got a raincoat, some wellies will do
If you haven't any wellies, bare feet will do
    If you haven't any bare feet . . .

Poor
old
you!

After the drought

At the end of the hot, hot summer of the big
   drought
there was – at last – a huge thunderstorm.

But the ground was so hard,
all the gardens and the parks
baked like brick,
criss-crossed with cracks,
that when the rain came
it didn't soak in.
It couldn't.
So it just ran away
down the hills
rushing like a river
splashing past the wheels of parked cars
bursting up over the kerbs

leaping round lamp posts
swamping the drains

and on down
and down
all the way
to
the
bottom.

And there
with the drains full up and nowhere else to go
the rain had a party on that hot, hot day.
It filled up the roads
pushed over garden walls
and gurgled and sang
while the children
swam in the street.

After that the council built a new storm sewer.
It was very big.

Fox

After dark
  when the cars park
    and the streets are quiet
Fox comes
loping calmly over the wall.

He strolls
  along the pavement
     and
       across the road
  with his long nose,
    sharp ears
      and his feathery brush of a tail,
flows like water through the shadows and hard
spaces.

He goes alone.
This is his place

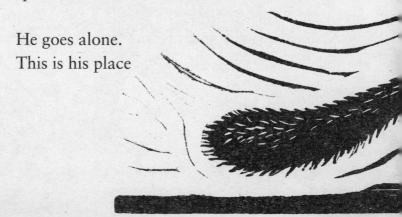

these trails of smells,
    the bins and bags that are his pickings
the yards and parks,
    back alleys and the hollows under cars.

If we pass by he turns and with one look
    reminds us
      that we've only borrowed it.

The car factory

First we roll out the steel,
   then we cut bits and shape them,
use robots to weld them
   and paint them and bake them.
We fix in the bits,
   all the lights and the wires
and the seats and the engines,
   the wheels and the tyres
and the glass for the windows
   and carpets – all there
while they're moving along
   on a belt in the air.
Then we check them and test them
   and polish and drive them
away to the dealers
   for someone to buy them.

Cars, cars!

They hum, they drone,
   they purr, they squeak,
They cough, they rumble
   and rattle and roar
They honk and hoot
   and groan and creak
Cars! cars! More and more!

Digger ditty

Did you ever see a digger dig a deep damp ditch
or a dozer digging drains in the road
watch the driver drag a lever
and the claw begin to heave
a great big heap of rubbish in its load
by any chance?

Look at the train!

Look at the train
Look at the train
Look at the train,
the train, the train!

Rattling by
Clackety-clack
at the back of the houses
up on the track.

Flickety-flick
Clickety-click
into the city
quicker than quick.

Over the bridge
And under the river
racketing on
for ever and ever.

Don't look at the wind
Don't look at the rain
Just look at the train,
the train, the **train!**

Rush-hour bus

A bus in the rush hour's
like a tin on wheels.
We all squeeze in
like keen sardines.

The train

The train swallowed my uncle
and it swallowed my auntie Jane.
   Oh no!
The doors opened wide,
they just stepped inside
and it snapped them shut again.

It raced off out of the station
like a great mechanical snake
   Whoooosh!
with hundreds of people
locked up inside
the world's worst bellyache.

It's vanished and so have my uncle and aunt
I don't know if they'll ever come back
   Oh dear!
And all that's left is a green signal
and a quivering silver track.

Sing a song of satellites

Sing a song of sixpence,
a necklace of pearl-like
spiky silver satellites
circling the world,

picking up our messages,
bouncing back our words,
reaching out where we can't see.
What have they heard?

Sing a song of satellites
a hundred miles high,
tons of hefty metal
weightless in the sky,

stretching out their tentacles,
gleaming in the dark,
giant silver insects
hovering on the margins.

Sing

    word catcher,

        weather watcher,

sun singer,

      star gazer,

map reader,

    war maker . . .

sing a song unknown.

Pylons

Where have the giants gone?
When did you see
any giants
like the ones they tell us
used to be?
Those were seven leagues tall
with seven hairy heads,
goggle eyes, dub clubs
and an appetite for eating
little children.

Did you see?

Across the motorway
and the railway,
over the fields they
stride.
Mile after mile,
block of flats high,
the pylons
hum to each other
like a chain gang
against the sky.

Feet in the cornfields,
feet on the hills,
they stand there
with wire hair
and scaffold arms
holding the line.

They wait
for you to go.
You wait
to see them move.

On the barbed fence under each,
child high,
hangs the sign
"Danger of life!"

Inside the wire

Yesterday I asked Charley
who's five
and good at plugs and wires
and sockets and things
what he thought electricity was.
'It's invisible fire,' he said.

'Look at the filament glowing
in the light bulb.'

'That's it!' I said,
Inside the wire
invisible fire
waiting at the switch to be let out.

Invisible Fire

It's everywhere.
Wildfire.
It's the sparks in your hair
when you pull off your jersey
on a dark, dry night.
It's the lightning spike
that rips the sky
and lets the thunder out.
It's the stingray
and the electric eel.

We tame it,
make it from oil and gas
and call it power.
We run it through
heavy cables in the air,
under the ground
and behind the walls.
Wirefire.

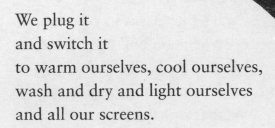

We plug it
and switch it
to warm ourselves, cool ourselves,
wash and dry and light ourselves
and all our screens.

Look at the fine wire
burning in the lit bulb.
It drives the shadows
to the corners of the room,
but it's too hot to hold.

It's invisible fire
and we are surrounded.

I must not play with sockets

I must not play with sockets.
I must leave the lights alone.
I must not pry into the wires
that lie under the floorboards
and run along
inside the walls
but
they can't keep the words from me.

And
if they can't keep the words from me
I can make things of my own.
I can cast electrical spells
        say a plug and a cable and a junction box,
        a clip and a fuse and a ceiling drop,
        a bulb and a transistor,
        a transformer and a switch
for I am an electrical witch!

George the plumber

George the plumber was a fine sort of man.
   He was tall and he carried a heavy bag of tools.
   When he came he took the house apart
   and underneath the walls
   he showed us
         pipes!

Now there were long ones and curly ones,
         angles and bends.
There were some going up, he said,
         and some coming down
           (I couldn't tell the difference)
'If you take up the floorboards like this,' he said,
'you can see them go this way and along there and
   through
and right at the top there's a tank,' said George.

So now the boards were up and the plaster was
   down
and the water was off (turned off in the road)
and George the plumber pulled out pipes,
long ones and twisted ones like iron spaghetti.

Then George the plumber took a special pipe bender,
    it weighed a ton on two iron legs
    half a wheel at the top and a handle and a lever
and the shiny new pipes,
the straight copper tubes, were
soon bent round corners and on their way.

He had them up the walls and under the floors,
he fixed them to the tanks and the taps and the drains
        with a blow lamp's flame.
Now they're hidden again
and George the plumber has put back the boards
        and mended the walls
                    and gone.

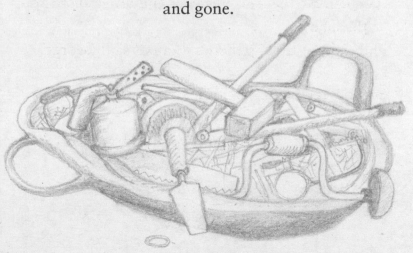

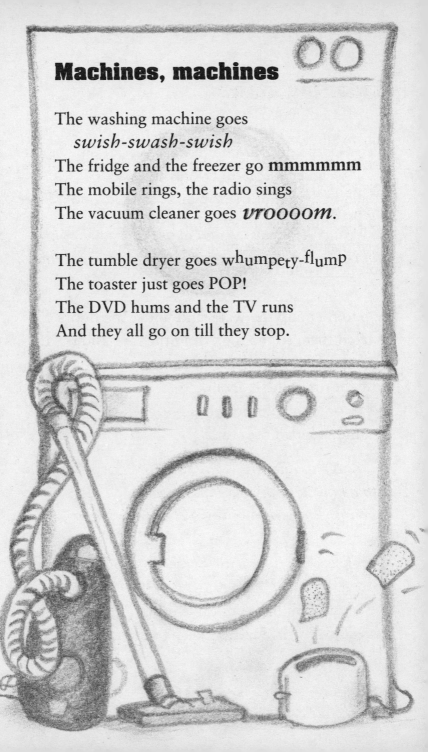

Machines, machines

The washing machine goes
   swish-swash-swish
The fridge and the freezer go **mmmmmm**
The mobile rings, the radio sings
The vacuum cleaner goes *vroooom*.

The tumble dryer goes whumpety-flump
The toaster just goes POP!
The DVD hums and the TV runs
And they all go on till they stop.

Under the stairs

You've all heard of unicorns, giants and witches.
You've heard about spaceships and aliens from Mars.
You've heard of lost kingdoms, explorers,
    enchantments
. . . *Well, now let me tell you about the load of old*
rubbish that we keep putting into the cupboard under
our stairs.

There's a pile of odd shoes, outgrown boots,
    broken roller-blades.
There's a buggy needs mending, a shopping bag
    with wheels.
There's a backpack gone mouldy, crash helmets,
    a milk crate
. . . *And a toddler tricycle, 2½ umbrellas, a straw hat*
with a hole in it, my old lunchbox and . . . do I need
to go on? I'm sure you've got the idea by now.

Mum keeps the door shut. Someone else leaves it
    open.
The cat went in once but came out pretty fast.
It's really quite strange, we keep putting this stuff in

*. . . And we never take anything much out again and
yet it never seems to get full up.*

The last time I passed the door was ajar
And the weather was bad and I'd nothing to do
So I thought I'd go in there and hide and surprise
    them
*. . . Besides, you never know, there might be
something interesting among all that stuff.*

So I stooped to get in past the junk, it was dark,
I crawled and I crawled for what seemed like an age
Till I came to a place with a space to sit down
*. . . And then I sat down and waited for a bit while
my eyes got used to the darkness and THEN what do
you think I saw?*

Nothing! There was nothing! The floor was all bare!
Just a few twisted springs, strings and half-chewed-up
    things.
It looked more like a cave or some wild creature's lair
    than our cupboard.

*. . . And it was dark, really dark and it smelt horrible
in there and I couldn't work out where all the junk
had gone to. I mean, I know none of us had cleared it
out.*

Perhaps there's another door and someone just took
   the stuff.
Perhaps it got damp and all rusted to dust.
There must be some nice, easy, safe explanation . . .
   Mustn't there?
*. . . Because after all, everybody knows that there
are no such things as monsters, not rubbish-eating
monsters, I mean not in the real world, not under the
stairs, not in our house?!*

I'm sure something moved! I'm sure I heard
   breathing!
I'm sure I saw eyeballs shine green in the dark.
I was too scared to scream, I scraped and I scrambled
*. . . And I got out of there just as helter-skelter fast as
I could, crashing out onto the hall floor like a great
heap of jangling rubbish myself.*

I didn't say anything. I didn't want to scare them.
I thought they might laugh if I did anyway.
Now I just keep the door shut and do like the others.
. . . Chuck in the odd shoe,
an old football or two,
a hat with a hole,
broken curtain rail pole.

It's probably better to keep it well fed . . .

    Whatever it is . . .

        In there . . .

            Under the stairs.

Don't wake the monster

Don't wake the monster!
>The monster's fast asleep.
We've got to be fast if we want to get past,
>so *Creep Creep Creep*

The monster's big and scary
>and we are very small.
Keep out of the light, keep out of sight
>and *Crawl Crawl Crawl*

He's dreaming of eating that chocolate cake
>and we don't want him to know
that we are going to get to it first
>so *Tip-Tip-Toe*

There's smoke coming out of the front of his head
>and spikes sticking out of the top.
We're getting closer and closer now
>so *Hoppety Hoppety Hop!*

Just look at those scales on the sides of his legs
  and those claws that scratch and rip!
If we're going to get to the chocolate cake
  then *Skip* *Skip* *Skip!*

We're almost past the monster now
  he's just a big old lump.
We're not scared of the monster
  Thump *Thump* **Thump!**

You see. Here we are. Here's the chocolate cake.
Oh no! The monster's starting to wake!
He's stretching out his scrabblish claws.
  He's roaring out his terrible roar.
  His slobbering jaws are opening wide.

  He's coming to get you . . .

RUN AND HIDE!

Don't change your grandmother into a frog

Don't change your grandmother into a frog.
Don't change your teacher to a tree
or your sister to a rock
or Auntie Edna to old broccoli.
Be nice and straight and sensible
like me.

Don't turn the bath into Niagara Falls.
Don't turn your dad into a flea
or your brother to another
cos your mother might get bothered.
Just see reason and feel easy,
be like me.

Don't turn the house into a submarine.
Don't turn Uncle Harry into glue
or your cousins to baboons
or the backyard to a moonscape
or . . .

Oh no!
Not that. Please!
I don't even mind so much about the backyard . . .
but not meeeeeeeeee . . .

My grandma

My grandma wears big wellie boots.
She builds bonfires
at the bottom of her garden
and bakes potatoes in the ashes for us.

She travels all over the world to work
and she climbs mountains
and she can sing.

She makes bread that's better than cake,
plaits it, twists it,
bakes it in a flowerpot,
puts seeds on the top
and tells us funny stories about Mum
when she was young,
lets us play with her toys . . .

And she's always busy.
Even when she's not working
she's busy.
Can I be like her when I'm old?

Ma's ma

Ma's ma
is my grandma
and Pa's pa
is my gramp.
And Grandma's ma's
my great grandma
and Gramp's pa's pa's
great great grandpa.
Now his pa's pa's
papa's papa's
mama's ma's
grandpa's pa
is my great great great
great great great great
great great great
great
grandpa.

Great-great-aunt Elfrida

My great-great-aunt Elfrida
    in the days of hats and veils
    and gloves and long skirts
    and lots of things girls shouldn't, couldn't do,
        took a canoe
and paddled down the length of the River Danube
        by herself.

Through Germany and Austria, Hungary, Romania,
   Bulgaria
– all of it an empire then –
 to the reed-split delta's creeks,
    low in the quiet of the flowing water
    it took weeks and weeks
   in the hat and the long skirts and the gloves
       by herself
except
      for . . .

an egg
that she found, fallen out of a tree,
or maybe was given, no one can say,

but she hung it in a bag on a ribbon round her neck
        and after a while
– you've guessed –
it hatched out
        a pigeon chick
                which sat after that
                        on her shoulder
                                under the shade of the hat
and stayed with her
all the way
        to the sea.

Blue mouse

When my uncle Clem was ten,
my mum, his sister, said
that he decided to breed a blue mouse.
Yes, blue.
He got it right into his head.

Which meant
that his mice had to go with them wherever they went
and that was a long way, mostly on trains,
from one end of Europe to another
from England
where they lived,
to Austria
where they'd come from,
or France and Italy
where they'd been in between,
Clickety-clack along the railway track
some time in the 1930s.

And when the mice weren't up his sleeves or in his lap
– the ones that were going to make the blue babies,
   soon, for sure, just you wait –
he kept them in a shoe box
with holes in the lid for air
and put it up in the luggage rack above the seats
 opposite
where my mum, one day, watched it drip-drip-dripping
onto the hat of a very fine lady who was sitting
just underneath the box in the rack,
Clickety-clack,
oblivious.

And did he?
Did he what?
Did he breed a blue mouse?

Nearly.

We're going to have a baby

They tell me we're going to have a baby.
'Oh yes? When?
This afternoon? Tomorrow?
Where is it then?'

They tell me it's still inside Mum
and it's got to do a lot of growing
before it'll be ready to be born.
I can't see anything.

But ever since they told me
I find them looking at me
carefully
from time to time
when they think I'm not looking.
I haven't done anything!

Yes of course I believe them.
 . . . I suppose.

Expecting

I wonder who this baby will be.
Will it be a boy or a girl?
Will it have black or brown hair?
(It might even be fair.)

If it's a girl
will she
like football like me,
come and hide in the hole in the wall
by the bins
want to stay awake after bedtime
        talking?
(It could be a he.)

But how do I know it won't be
someone like that boy down the street
who won't talk to me
who scowls at the window
when I go by
and laughs when his horrible dog
makes me cry?
I wish I knew who this baby will be.

Hospital baby

They brought in the new baby
in a see-through plastic cradle
on wheels
with a blue label.
It looked just like the others
but it was my baby brother.

At the edge of the white covers
I watched his fingers curl
saw his blue eyes open
take in me and the world.
He gave a gigantic yawn
in miniature,
my very small
live baby brother.

Good night

Good night. Sleep tight.
Stay in your beds, all right?
No more creeping, no more crawling,
No more squeaking, whispering, bawling.
This is it! Put out the light!
Good night. Sleep tight.

Excuses

It's excuses, excuses, a million and more excuses.
It's the goodnight-stretching, parent-catching,
bedtime song.

There's
      'Don't shut the door, Dad, it's dark in here.'
and
      'Mum! Mum! I can't find my bear!
      I thought you said it was under my bed.'
and
      'I'm thirsty, I'm thirsty.
      Please can I have a drink of water?'
starting quiet and getting louder,
      'Please can I have a
      drink of can-I-have-a-drink-of
CAN I HAVE A DRINK OF **WAAAAATER!**'

Then there's
      'I feel sick.'
and
      'I thought you called me!'

'I forgot to feed the goldfish.'

and

'I just need a wee!
It must have been that drink I think.'

And – this is a good one –
'I heard a noise, Mum.
In our room.
A knocking in the house noise
it could have been a mouse noise
but it could have been a burglar!
Mum, will you come?'

And there's always one more.
You've just thought of it I'm sure.

Underneath the blankets

Underneath the blankets
down by your feet,
you know those crumbs that wriggle
and those wrinkles that start to creep
as you're falling asleep . . .
Are you sure that's the sheet
by your left big toe?
Isn't that prickly patch in the corner
beginning to grow?

You've got your arms here
your legs there
your body and your head
and there's something coming to get you
from the bottom of the bed.
Watch out!

Your hands have gone heavy.
There's humming in your ears.
Don't blink, don't breathe,
pretend you're not there

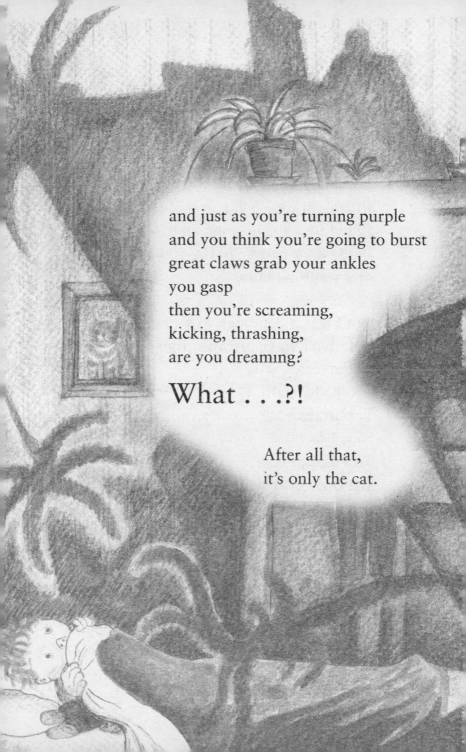

and just as you're turning purple
and you think you're going to burst
great claws grab your ankles
you gasp
then you're screaming,
kicking, thrashing,
are you dreaming?

What . . .?!

After all that,
it's only the cat.

When I was little

When I was little
but old enough to know
that night time is for sleeping,
I used to wake up sometime
in the dark middle of the night
and want my mum.

But I was old enough to know
you don't wake grown-ups in the night
not unless
it's really, really, *really*
important.

So I'd just go
trump trump trump
down the stairs from my room,
across the creaking floorboard
outside my mother's bedroom door
squeeeak
and into the bathroom
click.

And then again on the way back
out of the bathroom
onto the floorboard
squeeeeeeeeeeeeak
and there I'd wait
in my bare feet
just in case she happened to wake of her own
accord.

And if she didn't,
after a while
perhaps I'd just touch
her rattly door knob
but only lightly
because I didn't want
to wake her or anything.

And then sometimes I'd hear her sigh and say
"Come on, come and get in with me."
And then I'd open the door
and go into her room
and climb into her bed
and she'd turn over and go back to back
back to sleep
all warm
with me in the crook of her arm.

And sometimes she'd get up
and come to the door and say
"That's enough of that!
Come on. I'll tuck you in."
and she'd put me back in my bed
safe.

But sometimes,
sometimes she'd growl and roar
and chase me away with angry words.
And that was worse,
worse than everything,
even worse
than waiting alone in the dark
in the middle of the night.

So mostly I'd just stand there for a bit
Squeeeak Creeeeak
on that floorboard
until I got so cold
I just went back to bed again
by myself.

Lullaby

Hush-a-ba birdie croon croon,
Husha-a-ba birdie croon.
The sheep have gone to the silver wood
And the cows have gone to the broom, broom,
The cows have gone to the broom.

Traditional.

Pets, pets!

They're everywhere,
all over the place,
where you'd least expect
to see an animal face
appear, it's here.
It's as strange as it gets
but wherever there are people
there are sure to be pets.

White mice, hamsters, rabbits, rats,
horses, budgies, goldfish, cats,
turtles, lizards, snakes and frogs,
gerbils, guinea-pigs, ducks and dogs,
spiders, salamanders, marmosets,

Yes, wherever there are people
there are sure to be pets!

I've got to have a pet

I've got to have a pet. I must have a pet.
I don't know why but I think I'll die if I can't
    have a pet!

I'll settle for a possum, a mouse or an egret,
but I've absolutely, definitely
    GOT TO HAVE A PET!

I'm going to call it Snowy, Rumpelstiltskin or
    Dorette
and cuddle it and stroke its head and tell it
    not to fret.
I know there's mess and smell and noise but
    I won't be upset
because I've absolutely, definitely,
    frantically, desperately
got to, got to, got to, got to,
    GOT TO HAVE A PET!

Please phone 1234567!

Lost

We've put up a poster on every tree,
one in the vet's and two in the pet shop.
Our rabbit's escaped, our big black rabbit,
and we've searched and we've searched
and we really miss him.
And now we're waiting
day after day for the phone to ring...
    And it does.

On Monday it's someone who's found a black rabbit
except it's not quite black,
it's white and brown as well
and, no, it's a female
and they can't keep it much longer. Could it be ours?

On Tuesday there's someone else who's found a
rabbit. It's brown actually.
Thought it was worth asking anyway.

On Wednesday there's someone who's found
   a big, black,
yes definitely black all over, yes, and it's male.

There's just one small snag. It isn't a rabbit . . . .
    It's a guinea pig.

On Thursday and Friday nobody rings
and we're starting to give up hope.

But on Saturday there's a call:
someone who says her mum said she had to ring
because they saw our poster
and they had found a rabbit . . . .
Yes. A week ago. And, yes, he's black all over
but she didn't really think he's the one we're
    looking for
cos he's big, yes, but not that big
and besides, they've had him for a whole week
and he's really tame
and they really like him
and maybe he'd be happier with them anyway
or he wouldn't have run away?
And they can't bear to part with him
please could they keep him?

And then we know
it's our rabbit.

Mr Black'n'Yeller

My sister's salamander disappeared down the drain.
We never thought we'd see him again
but he was cleverer than we were,
Mr Black'n'Yeller,
turned up a whole year later
in the corner of the cellar.

The bad crab

The bad crab
ate the bacon rind.
She wasted the bait
and left behind
a wisp of weed
on my fishing line.

Bitten

Somewhere in this room
there's a fat mosquito
trying to fly
with a bellyful
of MY blood.
And I'm scratching, scratching, scratching,
scratching,
    scratching,
        scratching,
           scratching. . .

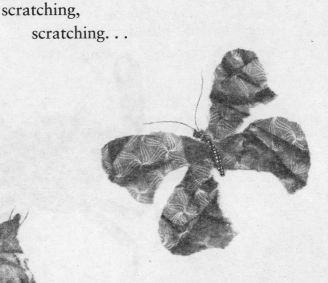

Moths

We let the moths in.
Somebody left the window wide open
it was a hot night
and there they were
spread-out wings against the white wall
all around the bathroom light,
small mottled brown
midnight moths

and the sound of loud voices
partying in the street beyond
seemed small
beside their waiting wings.

The lizard

The lizard darts
  Stop
      Start
head like a wedge
tail like a spike
  Solid
      Liquid
Solid again
Solar powered.

Who am I?

My head is flat.
My tail is fat.
My skin is dry.
My belly slides.
My tongue is split.
I hiss and spit.
I have no legs.
I'm long and lithe.

My eyes are small.
Make no missssssssstake
they see you all.
I am a . . .

Fizzer

We've got a cat.
His name's Fizzer
and he's wicked,
oh yes.

He's got this walk,
this slouch, slouch,
wiggle-your-bum,
look-at-me walk,
and these whiskers,
white spikes on a black cat,
in your face
just like that.
And what Fizzer doesn't know,
hey, nobody knows!

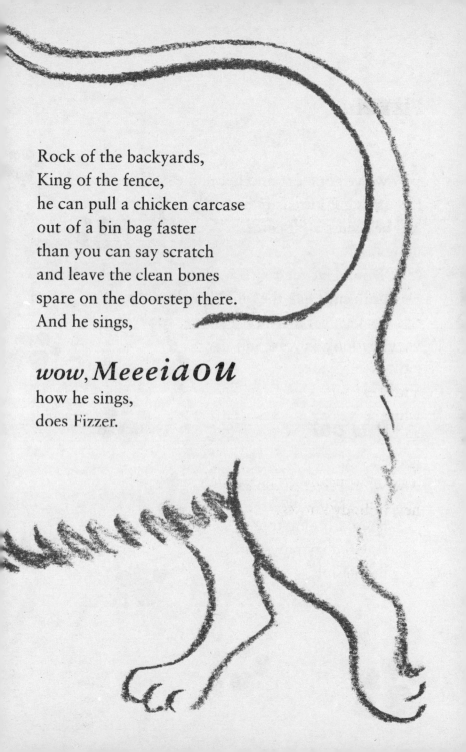

Rock of the backyards,
King of the fence,
he can pull a chicken carcase
out of a bin bag faster
than you can say scratch
and leave the clean bones
spare on the doorstep there.
And he sings,

wow, *MeeeiaOU*
how he sings,
does Fizzer.

Ellie

We've got a cat and her name's Ellie,
she's got kittens in her belly
yes, she's a fat cat.

'Don't give me that!
I can shift like the wind if I choose to,
so what's it to you if I snooze too?
Just look at you! Shoo.'

Our cat

Our cat drinks
from dripping taps
leaves dirty paw-prints
in the sink.

Silver

Silver the cat has work to do,
     sleeping.

In the day it's sleeping in the rocking chair
by the window where the sun comes in,
keeping a closed eye
on me at my desk
with an occasional sigh,
a stretching of paws and claws
before curling up again for more
     sleeping.

At night it's up on Annie's bed
sunk in the duvet beside her feet
waiting for sleep with an urgency
that chafes at the bedtime delays
like some fretful cat-nanny
    Hurry up, aren't you ready yet?
    Some of us have work to do . . .

    sleeping.

KATHY HENDERSON is an award-winning author and illustrator, as well as an artist and printmaker. Among her many titles is the modern classic picture book, *The Little Boat*, with Patrick Benson, which won the Kurt Maschler Award and was shortlisted for the Smarties Prize. She also wrote and illustrated *The Storm*, which was shortlisted for the Kate Greenaway Medal.

Her books for Frances Lincoln include the colour poetry collection, *15 Ways to Get Dressed*, which she wrote and illustrated, *Pets, Pets, Pets*, illustrated by Chris Fisher, and *Hush Baby Hush, Lullabies from Around the World*, illustrated by Pam Smy.

Kathy visits schools regularly, running workshops and performing her work. She lives in north London.

Kathy is available for school bookings through Contact an Author (contactanauthor.co.uk)

MORE GREAT POETRY FROM
FRANCES LINCOLN CHILDREN'S BOOKS

978-1-84780-366-5 • PB • £6.99

978-1-84780-367-2 • PB • £6.99   978-1-84780-398-6 • PB • £6.99